The Sea

WARREN HANSON

SCHOLASTIC PRESS

# of Sleep

ILLUSTRATIONS BY **JIM** La**MARCHE**

NEW YORK

LIBRARY OF CONGRESS CATALOGING-IN-PUBLICATION DATA

Hanson, Warren.

The sea of sleep / by Warren Hanson ; illustrated by Jim LaMarche. — 1st ed.   p.   cm.

Summary: Soothing text takes the reader on a bedtime journey across a peaceful and beautiful sea to sleep.

ISBN 978-0-439-69735-4 (hardcover)

[1. Seas—Fiction. 2. Sleep—Fiction. 3. Bedtime—Fiction.] I. LaMarche, Jim, ill. II. Title. PZ7.H198915Se 2010 [E]—dc22   2009032602

10 9 8 7 6 5 4 3 2 1   10 11 12 13 14

Printed in Singapore   46

First edition, September 2010

The display type was set in Fontesque Italic and P22Parrish Roman. The text was set in Deepdene H and Deepdene H Italic.

The art was created using acrylics and colored pencils on Arches watercolor paper.

Book design by Marijka Kostiw

For Cody and Lacey,
from a lucky dad
—W. H.

To the readers and tellers
of bedtime stories
—J. L.

The Sea of Sleep is calm tonight.

Calm and still.

Her quiet ripples tiptoe on the shore,

Kissing quickly,

Then run away again,

Slipping swiftly back across the sand,

Carrying away the footprints of the day.

The Sea of Sleep is ours tonight.

Yours and mine.

We sail here, cradled in our cozy boat.

But someone else is here

To share the peaceful beauty

Of these silver waves.

It is the moon.

And all the stars.

And the darkness,

As it wraps us in its loving arms

And holds us safe and warm.

Drifting. Floating. Lightly gliding

On the Sea of Sleep tonight.

Rocking. Swaying. Slowly sailing

On toward the morning light.

The Sea of Sleep runs deep tonight.

Deep and clear.

We see its secrets dancing there below.

Far below.

And the dreamy dolphins rise

And make gray rainbows

As they play beside our boat.

And we float beside them.

Then they disappear,

Down into the sea below

So deep and clear.

The Sea of Sleep sings songs tonight.

Whisper songs.

Her sweet and pleasing voice is barely there.

But we hear it,

And her music tells us all we need to know,

In a voice so soft and low.

And we love to listen as we sail the sea.

Drifting. Floating. Lightly gliding

On the Sea of Sleep tonight.

Rocking. Swaying. Slowly sailing

On toward the morning light.

The Sea of Sleep is blue tonight.

Blue and beautiful.

A deep, deep blue-blue borrowed from the sky,

With brilliant crystals winking on her fingertips.

These gentle jewels

Light our voyage home across the night.

The Sea of Sleep is very old.

Old. And wise. And kind.

Her ancient waters know that we are here,

Sweet and sleepy, floating through the night.

And she tells us in a murmur of the many little sailors

Who have sailed here, happily, upon the tide.

Over many years.

Over many and many a million years.

Drifting. Floating. Lightly gliding

On the Sea of Sleep tonight.

Rocking. Swaying. Slowly sailing

On toward the morning light.

And we drift away.

Drift, drift away.

Away, on the Sea of Sleep.